I0521318

Storylandia

The Wapshott Journal of Fiction

Issue 31

The Wapshott Press

Storylandia, Issue 31, The Wapshott Journal of Fiction, ISSN 1947-5349, ISBN 978-1-942007-26-5 is published at intervals by the Wapshott Press, now a 501(c)(3) nonprofit, PO Box 31513, Los Angeles, California, 90031-0513, telephone 323-201-7147. All correspondence can be sent to The Wapshott Press, PO Box 31513, LA CA 90031-0513. Visit our website at www.WapshottPress.org to learn more. This work is copyright © 2019 by Storylandia. The Wapshott Journal of Fiction, Los Angeles, California. Copyright © 2018 Dawn Cunningham and is reprinted here with the copyright owner's permission.

Storylandia is always seeking quality original short stories, novelettes, and novellas. Please have a look at our submission guidelines at www.Storylandia.WapshottPress.org or email the editor at editor@wapshottpress.org

Donations happily accepted at donate.wapshottpress.org

Many thanks to KM Warner for the editorial support.

Cover image by Anibus, https://bit.ly/2m6CcPR

Storylandia

The Wapshott Journal of Fiction

Founded in 2009

Issue 31, Autumn 2019

Edited by Ginger Mayerson

The Beasthood

By Dawn Cunningham

Table of Contents

This story was inspired by Max Ernst's *Une Semaine De Bonte [A Week of Kindness]*.

Acknowledgements: "the dog barks madly my way" first appeared online in *Shuf Poetry*.

"Dreams, in fact, are essential for survival. [...] If deprived of dreams, these animals would often die faster than they would by starvation, because such deprivation severely disrupts their metabolism."
Michio Kaku

The Beasthood

by
Dawn Cunningham

Prelude

I am the prosecutor who has brought this story to the attention of the public, who will give you the physical evidence to prove the truth of the Beasthood, who will have you see the thing beyond the media's perception as something science fiction. Let the press mock the story and give the exposure, I will give another view to allow people to decide for themselves. This story begins in a court room on June 21, 2010, where girls have come forth to expose the Beasts. The press has entitled the scandal, "To All Beast, We're Aware of You," with these wondrous lines attached:

In the course of defending Beasthood, the defense fails in proving the beast is tame. The letters smelled out causes for more to rise up against the beast and his rule. Letters mature into a coffin, suggesting neither can live without the other while killing each other. Those automatic writings and sketches by pencil or crayon etch out what a beast could never have. Coincidence confides in the hand, and at times the feet: a stirring heats from sole to soul, or from toes to dendrites. That one tear that falls is all it takes for the jury to weave their necks around the trunks so heavily planted by the defense (of course they were barren—everything is always black and white). Don't be confused by the edged-coloring. "The beast is tame," denies the prosecutor; "Watch the girl scrawl against the bottle beating in her chest." Who can hear the child climbing out into bodily change that the mind cannot keep up with? "Let the Beast out!" the girl cries, but the wood absorbs her words.

Beast is tame in the past and in the future, the defense would have us believe. But, to what beast does the defense contribute tameness? Words unwritten on black lines unbinding the social construct of dialogue, or history and science untying skirt laces to make future? These are the questions we must ask; or is there still a question floating airlessly beyond the tongue tip because too many are afraid to equate it? Such as, what does one eye see that the other doesn't or can the left hand actually do without the other knowing? Or, what mind is in control? Yes, these are questions to be asked as well, and the last question that cannot be forbidden: does color give clarity or blur the now distant reality?

I've forgotten to show you that the jury, in their snail-gnawed shine and loose jaws, is wobbling to swallow without tongue or fluid. What does this trial search for among the buried? Not a single dead can speak to discourse of confusion made by a trap. Occasionally, there's a crack in the cage, and a little of what can't be spoken awakes with a pencil and a blank sheet. But the blood can't be forgotten; it isn't all gone, not yet. If it doesn't run through walking flesh, it runs through wormed-soil and clubbed-feet snaking down to the source. The dead have broken the code without lead in hand.

The defense, though shaken by that tear, gives notice to the dead that all of us carry a beast; such as the male Beast that he has us stare at. He notes: "Notice the Beast in his search for the mate so needed, and yet so distant. What possession does the mate have over the Beast and why is the mate unwilling to possess the possessive?"

The by-product of believing the Beast is tame is the unconscious searching for the coincident and the release of automation to squeeze tighter the logic with the senseless, the smell to the object, the vision to virtual reality walked in, slept in, and eaten in. How many spleens and intestines must be pulled out to see the lie engraved on the word Beast; on the word tame? Does either have meaning in birth or death? We are born beast and die tame, I've heard it said; but it also can be said that we are born tame and die beast because we are separate from nature by our own nature to tame the Beast. In doing so, we bury part of us.

The defense goes back to those letters to show the tame ways, but the prosecutor asks, "When letters are read by those not intended, or written to the dead, what is the difference?" I have an answer for the defense (for this isn't what he'll agree to but should): Both have fallen upon no understanding, and gain knowledge without an apple core so needed to plant deep in the soil mulched by beetles and paws and noses.

But we as the viewer cannot forget to ask about the witness's involvement with Beast and tameness. She has concealed her own true nature, snaring many in her timeless life. Is she a product of herself or of others— namely male? Does she service the female or the males by sitting on the white line that divides the crevice in steepness? Is she a woman, a Beast, or neither? She is more than the lion or tiger in wait. She is part of us and not of us, she is there and not there, she exists and doesn't exist, she encompasses everything that all wisdom fails to find; she is past, present, and future in the now. But aren't we all?

I'm unable to directly answer all the questions I have asked—I don't know you, and know you all too well to even suggest an answer for you. There will always be a part known only to the heavens (the cosmos, the stars, the planets, the gaseous bulbous fluid balled into itself). It's funny, that girl with the tear knows more than you and me!

I've given you the facts as they are in this court about whether the beast is tame. I can suggest (so you may answer the questions I've left unanswered) that you view your dog or cat, your horse or cow, yourself and mate against bookends, and sketch the unknown. It may define whether the beast is tame; and if it doesn't, don't worry about it, all of this doesn't mean a thing; nor the colors protruding (or escaping) focus. ~ Deloris Jaguer

After Ms Jaguer's wonderful view of this scandal, I enlisted her to follow along and to investigate. These are the findings brought to the courtroom, posted on Ms Jaguer's blog, or published in the local newspaper.

The Evidence...

Exhibit 1a: Cisci Loop Bed & Breakfast Contract, April 20, 1828:

This is one contract of many signed by every woman who entered the bed and breakfast, which indicates women signed their signature in blood. A bloody thumb print (slightly faded due to the many years of exposure) lies within the area between the tenant's signature and the part of the contract in red. The portion of the contract that appears in red is slightly faded, as well, compared to the upper portion of the contract written in black; chemical testing has shown human proteins exists within these letters.

Cisci Loop Bed and Breakfast Contract Welcome. *Please respect the rights of all boarders when visiting or staying.*

Cisci Loop is the owner of the Bed and Breakfast. Cisci Loop calls herself 'a' product for women's use. I, Cisci Loop, acquire from you, the tenant, the utmost secrecy of what you see and hear here, for yourself and others, and require that no man enters upon these grounds without prior written permission from me, Cisci Loop, for the sole protection of self and others that live and visit here. Within the written permission, you will find the path that will be taken to and from your apartment for the gentleman caller, as well as the food and drink allowed for the day of visit. You will also abide by leaving your door open when a male caller is present, once again, for your protection and others.

Signature: <u>Adorra Rose</u>

Date: <u>April 20, 1828</u>

With the above said, and upon your signature on this formal contract, along with a blood print of your thumb, further instructions for the function of your room will appear and be discussed.

Welcome to Cisci Loop's Bed and Breakfast, where I will help you thwart the Beast lurking at your heels, where I will teach you how to survive and hide from the long claws they grow to ensnare those of you who have come to me in hope of escaping the wild romance of promise, of pleasure and ecstasy, and the want of protected danger promised by such beast, or to be taught how to handle such activity, allowing complete survival and independency; thus, you in control, not the Beast, who lusts after feminine wiles needing guidance as a child. As it is in the Animal Kingdom for the Queen, the dam, the female rules the house, deciding upon all that shall be done. To be hunted is glorious, glamorous, exhilarating for the woman who is found worthy by the Beast. However, for the woman who is found worthy comes great loss of self if not prepared, if not taught the way, if not strong enough to keep the self intact as change occurs.

Your room is personally made for you, to protect you by desensitizing the effect of the male (the Beast) visitor and any item that the Beast may send to you. I remind you, the Beast in chase is unlike any male you have encountered. Do not ask how the room is personalized to your needs, nor ask how the room can desensitize the Beast or any item from the Beast, only know that no harm can come to you while within these walls. Also, remember, there will always be an "escort" within the Bed and Breakfast at all times, an "escort" to ensure the Beast leaves upon your command, an escort to do as you please to the Beast if the Beast feels a need to be excessively "affectionate." What can be done will be discussed in time, as well as taught to you, with the aid of an "escort." The "escort" is always on call, and will be at your side with one simple word: "BEAST."

Any violation of the rules here laid out within these walls will result in your immediate departure. Mind you, safety is my, Cisci Loop's, utmost thought and responsibility for those who find themselves on these premises. Those activities you do outside of these premises are not my concern, nor shall I question these activities, with the exception of sharing knowledge of fellow tenants whereabouts and what takes place within these walls. You may guide any woman to me that appears to be in need, but remember, you must not be specific to how I can help and protect.

The first rule, and most exclusive rule, to be abided by is the absence of sharing information with callers, and those outside of the house who inquire of roomers. If asked where a housemate rooms, other than to say the Bed and Breakfast, no information is to be given. This is knowledge not to be given under any circumstances; send those individuals to me.

If you can keep the first rule, the other rules will not cause problems for you. When you are prepared to lose yourself to the Beast, arrangements will be made to finalize the transformation. If you wish to complete such act without my assistance, pack immediately: no notification is needed. If you feel the need and know you are not prepared, wishing to protect yourself, call for an "escort." An "escort" will assist you in fighting off the want or need if you are yet prepared to deal with the fall, if you are yet prepared to be the Master Mistress of the relationship. You are in control here.

You may return at any time after leaving the premises. The room is always yours until the final contract is fulfilled: Total absence of the Beast upon your well-being or the decision to be forever with the Beast.

Best Wishes on the Journey before You

Cisci Loop,
Manager of Bed & Breakfast,
Womanhood of Humanity & High Priestess.

Cisci Loop, April 20, 1828

Exhibit 6: Journal of Winter Woods, October 08, 1833 through unknown date

A part of a journal written by Winter Woods who occupied Apartment A. This journal was found among a vast array of several papers, on the homestead of the Bed & Breakfast. On the journal was written "belongs to the occupant of apartment A" followed by her name. October 08, 1833

My words cannot spell a creation fallen from the sky. The rain drains into my eyes leaving them dry. I cannot touch my heart to cease the pain. I cannot write my brain into ceasing the thought of being a universe of him. HIM. Such an insignificant word for the creature who calls out for my blood to mingle with.... The left hand is a remote coast of a summer's first pudding. My right hand traces lava flow entering the mouth of... where wheat fields are depleted and plundered continuously, like the seasons done in one day.

November 30, 1833

Time no longer exists. I'm not here. Within this room are only shards of papers with letters scattered. Dates mean nothing. I cannot make sense of what happens some days. I put the lounge in the northeast corner to find myself misplaced in time, far back, long before the pilgrims visit. The southwest corner is where people who visit know me, I know them, and we are strangely dressed, but it is not me. The corner I enjoy the most moves quickly. I hide in this corner for several days, visiting distant places I've only dreamed about, traveling to them in the briefest of time. Huge birds that do not flap, huge birds made of metal, like our knives and guns. It is my imagination. I have asked Cisci about this. She only answers, "Anything is possible." What I don't understand are her words: "When you are ready, choose your space, choose where you belong. Here or there is your decision." Always the same words.

January 16, 1834

The creature that hungers for me has called upon me. Cisci says I am strong. That is why he pursues. There is something intriguing about him. I read my first entry. I still sense all the confusion and passion, and the 'want' he brings out in me. I dislike this affect.

Tea cup sea side in my head doesn't swallow a pheasant whole. Feathers have no tickle in my heart. I can see Paris in black. Black. HIM. He is the black of the black.

What is the date? My walls look like Christmas

It will not be long before I can leave here. Cisci says I'm the strongest of all her tenants. I must agree. The screams I hear coming from some of the apartments, and not always female, not always human.

Today, the creature called again. I faced it. I didn't linger. When he refused to leave, I called for the escort.

Why are my walls...? Nothing I've added since early December appears; where is... where are... damn, I can't remember what it is called; all those articles and photographs of... gone! And letters I opened and threw away are on my desk unopened?

I can't be sure of any date now.

The only use for the BEAST is in my beautiful majestic words that spill forth when he is near. I will keep a part of this feeling to warn others in my writing. Cisci said more will hunt me but my writing wards off the smell. I will keep writing and teach others.

My favorite corner is where I will go. I have come across a Beast there, a Beast who is pursuing a young woman whom has potential outside of 'breeding.' I have figured out what these Beast want. Breeding is only part of it.

Why does my friend Adorra wish to stay? She visits her apartment little. I've warned her of the young one who lurks about. I do wish to bid her goodbye and safety before my departure.

Exhibit 2a: Letter to Adorra from Cherrish, September 11, 1834

The first of letters in a series written to Adorra Rose, a onetime tenant at Cisci Loop's Bed and Breakfast. These letters were found among other papers of Cisci Loop's. It is not understood why Cisci Loop would have these letters; nonetheless, they were found gathered by a tied ribbon.

September 11, 1834
Dear Sister,

You must come home. Mr. Cougar has been asking for you. He is very ill, and the doctor believes your presence will do him good. I never did understand why you left. He loves you very much, and I thought you loved him. He speaks of you often. Last night he held a dinner party in your honor, to your return. It took much out of him, and his face, his eyes, were very down trodden. I didn't think he would be able to entertain. Many women advanced on him. He warded them off, thinking only of you. We talk often, but he will not tell me what it was that made you run. Please come home, just to brighten those eyes of his. It is sad to see him this way. When he hears your name he brightens, only to sink back into the deepest depression. This party brightened the house, for the curtains were pulled back, and still are—this gives me hope.

I'm writing this letter against his judgment. He

says you must come to him of your own free will.
    Love,
    Your Darling Sister Cherrish
    XOXO I miss you!

Exhibit 3a: Letter to Uncle from Vlad
December 07, 1834

The series of letters from nephew to uncle were found in the home that Adorra Rose was to inherit in Boston, Massachusetts. The exact location is not available for the courtroom or jury.

December 07, 1834
Dear Uncle,

    This day is the day I begin to share, slowly, the secrets of the house, the secret she has sensed since the moment she has arrived. I promise you, Uncle Cougar, that I wouldn't keep My Lady in the dark for long, not as you did to Your Lady, for it may make the situation more stressful than it will be already (like yours)—if only My Lady was not the daughter of you. Unlike others of our kind, I searched wisely, and was patient, waiting for the right lady of the house to expose herself to me: My Lady. Uncle, her mother concealed her well, and her sister as well, deep in the timbers where the wild beasts are, where the scents are unclear, blended, unless one has kept thyself well trained in the hunt. Not many of us are trained anymore, in the wild—you know that, that is why you forced me to become skilled in the 'true' hunt; so many of us have stepped into the modernization, forgetting where we have come from, forgetting what we are. You are right, someday our kind will be gone if we continue in this way.
    Your Dear Nephew Vlad Lyion

Exhibit 5a: Manifesto: Warning! Dancing Girl of Apartment G, December 30, 1767

This document was found between the pages of a young lady's diary, where she mentioned she found the long paper posted on the fencing to the Bed & Breakfast. The name of the young lady is faded, leaving only a few letters of identifications: *o, uti, Pop, se.*

December 30, 1767 Warning! Dancing Girl of Apartment G

I don't know where to begin this story of my visit with Miss Waters; it happened so quickly, so quietly, before I knew what was happening. . . and vaboom! there she was! standing in the naked flesh of sin before my eyes, dancing, bowing before me, throwing flowers from a basket.

I don't know how. I don't know why. She was just there. I slapped my face, thinking I was dreaming, closed my eyes, rubbed them till I thought they would fall out!

"Come with me," she repeated, until that was the only words I heard.

I had been in a bar that night, I think, at least I think we had gone to a bar that night, it looked like a bar I entered before... before it all started. I don't remember putting no more than one shot of vodka to my lips, I'm sure of it, and I definitely don't remember walking, crawling, or being carried out.

The stool was still under me, and the shot glass was still in my hand and somehow, someway, it was always full, never emptying as I drank more and more and more. My eyes never faded, never dried, my words were never slurred, the liquid tasting as mulberry one time, Scotch the next, and a delightful flavor I can't name; I've never tasted such a substance as this. Rich, smooth, a hint of rum, and a bitterness that somewhat resembled a tangerine—just a nip of it.

When I tasted this exotic flavor, the girl moved quicker, gyrating, twirling, feathering the petals from her fingers to enclose her body in a perfect circle, a perfect circle! I couldn't touch her, and I tried to move from the stool as she kept saying, "Come with me." Never once did I touch her. With each turn her face changed, the feature more slim or full, her hair plum, red, auburn, black, brunette, dishwater blonde, strawberry blonde, platinum blonde, her eyes deep as the sea, black as an onyx, greener than a pine, golden brown, a copper, hazel of hazels, a blue so blue they were violet, her cheeks high, low, large, hidden, her chin defined as a witch or smooth as a baby's bottom, cleft, flat, her nose a ski slope or flat against a window, upturned or hooked, ridged, humped, wide or thin, each face circulating like a casino slot machine, never the same face twice.

I know this isn't a believable story, and I still don't believe it myself.

You've seen those movies with rooms full of pillows and scarves, psychedelic colors, black lights dimming and brightening slowly, much slower than the music, of which had a beat to match the flavors I drank; and did I tell you each drink smelled as it tasted? The room and the music had its own smell as well and each time the woman approached me it swelled up and enveloped me in a thin bellow fog, clear fog, a fog I could feel, so clear it was like watching pin-sized ice crystals dance and shatter, driving into my flesh—without pain; my naked body!

As I realized my nakedness, a fat bearded man thundered in as an elephant, "Enough," clapping his hands twice, stepping at me with fingers pointed up, palms out toward me, covering my eyes.

I found myself, when I opened my eyes again, sitting on the bar stool, still holding a full shot glass, leaning on the bar, staring into a mirror that had colors fading slowly, disappearing; my clothes—I could feel it!—growing from my skin, reality growing with my clothes to see myself in the room of Blossom Waters of Apartment G, staring into my eyes!

She's a witch, a gypsy, a prowler... do not mingle!
Trey Panthaur

Exhibit 2b: Letter to Adorra from Cherrish, February 24, 1835

February 24, 1835

Dear Sister,

I was exuberant in seeing you, as was mother, after your last visit two years before. Your return made her alive; but you left so abruptly that day. What was wrong? Won't you speak to me? Mr. Cougar expects your return any day again, and waits. I think he wants to marry you. Miss Tossil has tried to catch his eye. I overheard her speaking to him, making snide remarks about the way you have treated him. I must agree on one thing, your actions leave things open for gossip. Anyhow, Mr. Cougar thwarted her advancements, detouring her thoughts into starting a shelter for widows—or more less, made Miss. Tossil think it was her idea. The Old Hill place, the one left abandoned, that will be renovated.

Love,

Your Darling Sister Cherrish

P.S. My friend in Indy visited today. He said something very odd. You don't live at this address. The resident acted as if my friend had lost his mind. Why would they lie? Or have you moved? Let me know.

Exhibit 3b: Letter to Uncle from Vlad, March 16, 1835

March 16, 1835

Dear Uncle,

Your love for the instinct detected what was ahead: My Lady's mother being of the blood as you, as me—I can see why you persuaded me to search her out, to bring her back to Boston. She is beautiful: her eyes aqua green, a glow that our kind can't resist; her skin a hint of gold; her hair dark clay and curled down her long neck. Your daughter, Darling, is much like Your Lady, except for those steadfast sapphire eyes. But, I'm sorry to say, I can't persuade Your Lady to return again, and definitely not with your daughters. If Your Lady knew about Darling and me? Still I write, if only for the record of my work. She named them well, Darling and Precious. I found, in Darling, a perfect mate, one who can partake of the feast, for her skin rises to the far off cry of instinct—though she does not understand all yet, as when Your Lady, Adorra, began to feel it, began to change. How did she escape you? How did she escape the same fate as the others? I will not let My Lady escape!

Your Dear Nephew Vlad Lyion

Exhibit 3c: Letter to Uncle from Vlad, April 13, 1835

April 13, 1835
Dear Uncle,

 I am at Your Lady's mercy. I may have to protect the second of your children from others like us. Why did you make me keep this promise with your blood, to do as she says? It is such a great responsibility I should have never taken. What a curse that promise has become.

 Your Dear Nephew Vlad Lyion

Exhibit 3d: Letter to Uncle from Vlad, October 05, 1835

October 5, 1835

Dear Uncle,

Oh, how you wanted to see your daughters! I'm sorry I failed. You knew conception had taken place, both times; and each time Adorra ran from you. You said the scent was strong on Adorra when she returned that brief time many years ago: strong with the scent of a recent birth, a female birth—you were right! Tell me, how did you know the difference? If only you could answer me, write me. And then to know Adorra had conceived again! The pain in your face as you spoke of your love the night I left; the pain in your body as you died for your love's touch, and for the child already borne. To think of that night we spoke. I wanted to take your weak body with me as I searched for your love, so you could see her! so you could claim her as you should have. I wonder, will I know when my mate conceives?

Your Dear Nephew Vlad Lyion

Exhibit 1b: Letter to Adorra from Cisci, Jan. 27, 1836

Jan. 27, 1836

My dear resident, Adorra Rose, Apartment B

I stepped into your vacant room. The scenes of your past haunt this room. I doubt the room will ever be available for another. This place will always belong to you, and your offspring. I ask that you carry on here after my time, and until then, help others find their way here, as we have discussed previously. The qualities you have displayed are a great asset to both worlds that must be served, but an even greater asset to the world for female humanity. It is your job to search out those women who are hunted for the special blood they possess. As you well know, the disease is not passed on from mother to child as we first thought. Contraction of this blood must be identified. First to find a way to stop it in the female and then to stop it in the male, which is most definitely traceable in all family lines. New breeds of this disease occur when the blood runs dry in areas. I have greatly appreciated your assistance in the research. I only wish we had the abilities to further advance our studies. If it was as simple as stepping through a portal, but it is not. I have been able to pass on some information to others, who have been able to reply on occasion. But this will come in time, as you know; we are not meant to leave our space as yet, and I may not be able to before my time has abated me. You, however, have many years before you. You may be on your own for a short time, until another is strong enough and able to be trained, as you, but I am sure another of your magnitude will come along in a reasonable amount of time. For now, care for your daughters. I only wish you would be open with them, prepare them, or at least enlist them under my care to aid them in the decision they must make, soon, very soon. I fear you have already lost Darling.

You understand I serve two sides: protect and serve the Womanhood of Humanity, and as High Priestess for the Beasthood. There are those who are never ready, and I must weed them out; there are those who are in a state of confusion, which need guidance to decide what is right; and there are those that have the strength to be Beast. It is a fine line we practice. While it is my goal, and soon to be yours, to find the means to defeat the disease that first ravished men, I must serve the Beasthood to keep death limited. Darling has come to me, just recently, to "transform."

Vlad Lyion waited at the gate. I also sensed Lionel Leapird; I could smell his odor upon Darling, along with Precious. Cornelius has no doubt sent them to take his daughters. I ask, why do you leave them to fend for themselves? Have I not taught you otherwise? Did you think you had more time? Did you think you could hide them? Please, respond quickly, I sense that Precious is beginning to change without a Beast at her side. During my last visit, Precious had a certain odor lingering about her. I'm sure you sense it as well.

Womanhood of Humanity & High Priestess,
Cisci Loop

As reported by Deloris Jaguer: Murmur: The Questions, June 21, 2010

As reported to me by Ms Jaguer while sitting in the courtroom, overhearing a conversation through the murmurings before the afternoon break ended (June 21, 2010).

Murmur: The Questions

Woman in a dark pant suit: "What is this?"

Man, next to her, who she spoke to while waiting in the hall: "Don't you believe?"

Woman: "Anyone could have written those letters and those journal entries."

Man, smiling intensely: "The coloring of the paper doesn't make you believe?"

Woman, chuckling: "No. It can be faked."

Man: "You don't believe the experts? The defense and the prosecutor both agree the pieces are authentic. Are you telling me both are lying?"

Woman: "Could be."

The two sit silently for a bit. The young lady being questioned is dressed in semi-retro. She looks as if she has confused her eras.

Woman: "This is an occult."

Man: "Is it?" He looks right into her eyes. She stares, then leans back from his face.

She begins to speak, only to hold her tongue.

He watches her closely, smiling, enjoying the

reaction he is creating in her.

She fans herself. Her skin begins to redden, as if her blood is heating up: "Excuse me sir," she stands, sliding between him and the back of the bench before her. He takes in a large breath through is nose, smelling her as she goes by.

She is not wearing perfume. I do not know what he smells.

Exhibit 7: Journal of Leopold Lynks, April 19, 1754

This Exhibit is from a young man who fought the beast within him. This particular journal entry is from Leopold Lynks, a young gentleman who locked himself away. This journal was found buried in the basement of the home he once owned between the base of Blue Mountain Ridges and Blacksburg, Virginia. He was an intelligent man. Intelligence is one of the traits for these beasts: natural intelligence that leads to academic intelligence. This is the last entry.

April 19, 1754

    I really doubt this journal will ever be found; if it is, it will be tossed or burned because I'm crazy. I truly hope this well-kept journal finds its way into the hands of someone who can help others or who is in need of help. Whatever I have, I have come to call it Cat Fever. When I first noticed the symptoms of wanting to hunt—without a weapon—like a wild animal, getting down on all fours to run and chase, I began to wonder more about the other "symptoms." I'm young and intelligent. At the age of 15, I began to attend New College in Massachusetts. Few colleges boasted about chemistry, and this is what I wanted to study. Eventually, I would be led into anatomy because of my "condition." The closest I could get to the study of anatomy that I wanted was at College of William and Mary but I didn't want to move, and I didn't. I began to study on my own between classes at New College, which I finally had to leave in my junior year due to my "condition." I could no longer control this incredible urge to sniff at women, especially beginning at their... there is no polite way to say it, vagina. When this would come upon me, I could feel facial features beginning to change. There was one young lady who said my face started to look like a lynx. I was taken aback by this statement. I started to study the feral animal. I found many of my traits were similar to what I read and what I observed when taking off into the mountains—missing many many days of school. I had no doubt I had "cat" in me. I could say I left school but it came down to being dismissed. I was packing my things, readying to depart a week prior to the dean approaching me. The school did try to help me. Finally, I knew it was time to go after nearly attacking Miss Prudence Applebee in the classroom during an intense test. Her nervousness and sweat drove me insane. I wanted her right there, no matter who was watching. I left school for three weeks, visiting my feral friends, where I was very comfortable.

I've kept this a secret, even from my parents. At times, I want to dissect myself to find out what is inside of me. With the few friends that I have, some help me experiment, work through my theories with me. They are good friends. They have not told anyone. I'm hoping my journals get into the right hands. Steve promised to take my journals (if he reached them before anyone else) after my death and to keep them safe.

This morning, I experimented with a garment from a woman with a name that fits a pattern I have figured out. Once again I watched myself change form.

I've started to look into blood samples of these various women. It isn't the name alone. I don't have to know the name of the woman of whom the garment belongs. I always know she is what I want just by the smell. And each of these women have names similar to Prudence— something to do with beauty or quality character and surname attached to nature. Joseph is doing ancestry research on these women for me. I'm afraid to leave my secluded place between the edge of the mountain and the nearest civilized city. In the evening, I lock myself in the dungeon I have built. During the day I barely leave the security of my home, keeping the curtains closed, even way out here. I only go out when my friends are here. I don't feel safe otherwise. It isn't my safety I worry about.

If only there was another like me, another man that I could study, his reactions, take note of his thoughts he was willing to share with me.

Tonight will be hard for me. Something is coming. I can feel it. The area feral sense it too. Steve and Joseph wanted to stay to help me get through it. I refused. Whatever is coming isn't good.

The mirror stares at me. I'm changing. I leave this journal here for Steve to find if... if something happens to me.

Exhibit 2c: Letter to Adorra from Cherrish, January 30, 1836

January 30, 1836

Dear Sister,

 Mr. Cougar is bedridden. He will not see any person, not even the doctor. I had to force him to allow the doctor in. I'm surprised he even allows me to come and visit. But he has me read your letters to him, the letters you wrote when traveling; they comfort him. After I read a letter, I see a small shine in his eyes. What have you done? What did he do? I'm afraid if you don't come soon he will die. The doctor says there is nothing more he can do for him.

 Love,

 Your Darling Sister Cherrish

Exhibit 3e: Letter to Uncle from Vlad, February 17, 1836

February 17, 1836

Dear Uncle,

I'm going to take it slow, now, so nothing goes wrong. My hope is to have your children in their home soon. I know this letter may not reach you before your passing; however, I will continue to carry out your wishes and record all for future references. Your Lady will take me some time to persuade, hopefully conquer, to bring back into the pride. She is strong, I will admit. Be assured, my promise will be kept. I don't want to get too close to her yet. Distance is important at this time.

Your Dear Nephew Vlad Lyion

Exhibit 4a: Monologue: Darling Speaks to Precious, October 01, 1836

This Exhibit is an account of a conversation passed down from mothers to daughters, each learning one piece of dialogue. The other half of the dialogue is missing due to the death of an old one before sharing the piece with her granddaughter, since she had no daughter of her own; however, what is here is substantial. The dialogue is performed at family gatherings each year. It is said the dialogue took place in a forest on October 01, 1836.

Darling Speaks to Precious

It is good to see you, sister. Let's walk among the timbers, the timbers that I left behind for another seclusion. I have much to tell. You have grown, Precious, into a lovely young lady, such beauty in your hair, your eyes, in your step. Your hair is somewhat darker than mama's, something that enhances your dark brown eyes. I'm surprised mama isn't keeping a closer eye on you. But her absence from the life she is supposed to lead is killing her. I think we have gone far enough. Here, let us sit among these logs, the ones that are moss covered; they will be soft.

Do not be a child; you have grown into a beautiful woman, do not spoil that sight.

I will tell you my tale of love, of travel, or lack of, of the sea, of romance. But I warn you, be prepared to not believe me.

No, I won't lie; everything I tell you is the truth. Just listen, you'll question me, Mama did, as I wrote her. I know she did not share those letters. They frightened her, as much as her realization of what she wrote her sister—the letters she did not send. Mama has never shared the letters with you, doesn't know that I have read them before she ever told me about them. She thought they would save me. Thus the reason she did not share them with you.

You read mama's letters? Good. So this won't make it any harder. And yes, I sent the letters to you. Mama must have hid them elsewhere, or burned them.

She is frightened, mama is, by what she doesn't understand, of what she ran from instead of facing, the beast within a man that makes him more than a man, that part of a man that most women cannot tame, that type of a man that searches for a mate to tame him, like us.

Are you ready?

Good? We are far from the village, I'm sure no one has followed. It is time I prepare you for a world much different from what you see here.

Different in many ways, and in some ways, not much. Some, like our mother, lonely, but loneliness is not for us. Now, listen closely, this life isn't meant for all women, only the strong. Mama wasn't strong.

My husband, before he was my husband, was intriguing in the way he spoke and the way he moved, much like a large size cat with an alley cat attitude. I could not imagine the power he possessed, at that time, above people and of money. I couldn't imagine it because of his talk, the way he spoke of life, the thrill of living directly off the land, the way he talked about the kill, the blood running from the mouth, and the wound, then the stripping of the intestines, as though he had done it a thousand times before coming here, before finding me. His beauty did not match the words stricken on his tongue. Blonde, beautiful honey highlighted by the sun, nothing like you find among the woodland's men, and eyes with an underlying blend of autumn red leaves in the brown. You remember?

I will never forget those words he spoke to the men, in front of me, in front of the church, "If you don't take all the intestine you will spoil the meat, poison it, and then what good has the kill been?" I thought maybe it was bar room brawl talk to impress the woodsmen here, so he would not look so out of place, or thought it was to impress me, to make me know that he could care for me, that he would live off of the land, eat opossum stew, and venison, sweet and bitter, wild and tame, all at the same time.

I know this isn't clear, what I speak of yet, but be patient, it will come, especially if mama has discussed some of the letters with you. I will ask you if you understand when I have spoken my tale. Please, now, be patient.

You know, that of all the girls in town, I wasn't quite naive, but then, I never fell to the city life, kept our secure woodland inner circle of a comfortable lifestyle to know there was a difference from how we lived with furniture carved from our own hands, and the pottery we spilled out by hand every summer to replace what we broke during the winter, or cracked by leaving it out for the animals to lap up the leftovers, or the food canned and stored during the summer for our winter meals before the greenhouse to the cushioned seats made in a building by many hands. You, I, have never had a person wait on us, buy us furs and furniture, so fancy with graphic designs. And with all of this being brought to me, I wondered, what was he doing here?

Why me? And remember mama asking me all the time, "Do you love him?"

I did not then; that wasn't what made me decide to accept his proposal. I was curious about the other world that you haven't seen yet, that you still haven't read about.

The only contact we had then was from the tightknit group mama kept us in, where the girls didn't want to know about the world outside the world they had. Spoiled, bratty, daddy's girls.

Mama did have a picture of Boston that I used to look at late at night when I snuck into her chest.

You've seen the picture? Good.

Mama showed it to you?

I'm sorry to hear that you had to see the picture under such circumstances. Mama must miss him, must be hurting for leaving him like she did. Maybe all this won't be so shocking, and still, mama wouldn't share my letters, give you that which was addressed to you. Remember what mama said to me before I left?

Well, she said, "I'm not sure if you should go with this man, should marry him. He's too worldly for the likes of you." Now understand, mama is not a bad judge of character, and still, I couldn't believe her, I had to see what it was I had been denied for years.

Before I knew it, I was stepping off the carriage, the chauffeur somber and blank, with lines written across his cheeks and forehead, as if the face was telling me a secret that the master held, that my husband kept hidden, that I shouldn't find, that I knew that I had to find.

Yes, a mystery, a mystery that would kill most women, which would have killed mama.

No, as I told you, mama's strength is not for this world.

There is more to my beastly man then his name, Mr. Lyion; and his manner, the words he spoke without flinching, the taste of the kill that should have frightened me then, here, before I left, and didn't, now awaken in me, making me fearful to step down, as though the puddle beneath my feet was the blood of many kills. As I looked out upon the view, I wondered, was this how the world lived, how the rich lived, secluded, as I did with nothing more than my own hands and my own wits? Where was the money? Wasn't money travel, friends, gayety, a house full of people and parties?

Now, please, be patient, show that lady quality from the inside that I see on the outside.

I accept your apology.

Now, where was I. Ah, yes. The house, the dreary mansion that is mine, my home, our home, the lovely white picket fence with the huge white house covered with black shudders, and adorned with gargoyles; my life, different only in that I would not make what I needed, and still alone, still locked up in the back corner of the woods by water, water that surrounds me, an island with a land of water to divide me from all those things I expected to see, to visit, to be in the world, to safety. But only for a time.

Oh, no, my darling sister, I was never in danger, actual danger; I was too cunning for the man who had taken me; I learned too quickly to be killed as prey, found a way to escape if need be, but waited, waited until I was ready.

As I stood on the foot lift, the figure of a man, my husband, lifted me up, out of the thought I carried then, and placed his bristled chin against the small exposed breast of mine, sending a tingle through me. Oh, to feel as this, at his touch, it had to mean I felt love.

And from above his head I saw for the first time, the real hair he grew, thick as the pelt of a mountain lion. His grasp became strong upon my ribs, and a purr escaped from between his lips, he nuzzling into my bosoms, breathing deeply. Another wave of fear flooded through me, I feeling as the prey... O! Feeling as the prey that has been captured to be played with before the meal. A meal that I had never partaken of, a meal that our mother never discussed with me, nor I and my playmates openly dreamed about, only whispered occasionally the obscenity of a kiss between others, the real feast, to be eaten by the other.

No, he never tried to devour me, never pawed me in any way that would have done harm to me. He is a gentle man, with an animal persuasiveness that is alluring, and dangerous for a woman that is not strong.

I cannot call out his name in public; it is not for others to hear his name; not to be spoken by any other than those he has chosen to speak it; and only in a whisper; only behind closed doors.

I know you do not understand, and understanding will come in time, but what is most important is to prepare you for the world out there, the world you will enter; I know you are much wiser than the playmates I have watched you dance with. Please listen, let me continue, then we shall speak of the questions that you have.

The first night in the closed up house, with thick curtains and fires roaring in large rooms, he took my hands, allowing me to touch him as I felt comfortable in doing, as we danced to some music he could only hear at first, dancing from room to room that first night. The sun was still up when he began his advances, and I asked why the house must be so dark, so dreary during the day, why the sun could not brighten our dance that we were partaking of. His reply was unusual, but I did not question him any further.

Oh, what he said was sweet and bitterly scorning all at the same time. "I do not want the sun to thicken the white flesh I prepare for the ultimate dinner; I do not want the neighbors to peer in and tell of our love during the day, or see the meal we share between our fleshes."

Yes, it was a romantic line, and a succulent line, a line that I should have ran from, the secret that I should have hidden from, but I kept on searching, I kept on dancing, stepping along with him in the music he could only hear. This frightened mama, and she asked that I come home; she insisted that my life would not last long, that I could not cuddle the creature that had stolen me away with his magical trance.

This is what frightened mama. I know it is, and since she was not strong enough she believed I was not. Mr. Lyion does have a way of putting you into a trance, making you want to search him out. I think mama knew that I would fall for him, that I would be lost to the beast, and become part of the beast, come to enjoy the beast, to be the beast.

Many nights we danced to the music he could only hear, and then, by the end of my first month stay, I started to hear the music, the rhythmic beating of hearts, the drums calling from the leather of animals stretched tight over open thighs. More and more I moved my hands over his body, not afraid, and strangely restricted, his body portraying unusual traits—at least from what I knew about a man's body.

Am I frightening you? Maybe I should go no further. I thought mama had spoken to you about a man's structure?

Then it is a panting in your eyes, the lust for

the touch, just from my speech. You will do fine in the world, but you must know how to control yourself, not touch what isn't yours. Take my warning with great heed.

That night, the night I felt no restraint, I pressed myself upon him; and he had a bed prepared for us, a bed that we would share; you see, we had not slept in the same bed, not even the same room, until I was ready; he allowed me to have control. Now, when he called his male servant in, to order the readying of the marriage chamber—the man that is his chauffeur is his personal keeper as well—had lines more quickened than they had been a month before, as if he had aged twenty years, and those eyes, those eyes of his, they frightened me more than my husband bedding me for the first time. I stared at him, he stared back, pleading with me, with those eyes, pleading me not to search for the secret hidden within the house, within the man I stood next to, the man that was my husband, and my husband glared at the servant, spoke without a word, cautioning him not to overstep his boundary, for I was not his to protect. All of this I knew by their eyes. It was strange, I could see the words form within my eyes, I could smell the intellect traveling between the two, an animal instinct that humans have forgotten. And in that interchange of no words, Mr. Lyion took my hand and twirled me, laughing, saying, "Soon the night will leave this house forever, the sun will shine by day and by night. The hunt begins, tonight!" I did not understand, and was now frightened by the idea of myself being given to him.

Don't try to hurry me; the story needs to be told with firmness and completion. The hunt is nothing more than acting out a man's need for power over that which is wild, to take down the prey. You must hear it all, then you will understand why I am here.

Shhh, listen, someone is coming. Let us move on, farther into the forest, where only the creatures can stir in my tale. I will speak quietly while we walk.

Remember your first time when you hunted? Your first kill? The butterflies you had, and the way you knew how the prey felt before dying? It is the same; except for death is not the same as the death you know. The death you will know is the beginning of life. There are three deaths: one is the loss of singleness, the second is the loss of oneness; the third is the loss of life. You will experience the first death with glee.

Here. Here, let us move farther out. I miss the Timber. October is beautiful here, all the time. I think we've moved far enough now. Let's sit next to the flowing stream, where the sand is mixed evenly with the soil, a soft and sinking comfortable seat to sit on as I finish what it is that you should know.

The chamber I was taken to was adorned with lilacs and lilies, the royal and the pure all in one room, and the bed clothed in silk sheets, pulled back to expose the velvet pillows underneath; the quilt sewn with gold thread, pushing the royal color to a head, fluffed like feathers of a hen that has been ridden by the rooster. And in this marvelous dungeon of a home was an indoor outhouse, called a bath closet. How wonderful it was to bathe from water flowing into your own bedroom! And a belly stove in the corner to keep you warm, and to warm the water, a bathing room of privacy. He did not try to enter. I know he listened to my delight, my elegant surprise of rose pedals placed in the water for me, the gown to be worn as a bride for the walk down the aisle, white with purple stitching. And after I had bathed, I could hear his breathing through the door, the inhaling, exhaling, as I lingered in the bath closet dressing for our first night, dressing in white lace that flowed from a silk body, draped across my rose nipples, that pressed out, excited and fearful of what lay in wait. His breathing, definitely growing into a rhythmical purr of a cat being scratched behind the ear, rose my nipples hard, becoming harder, moving with my heart beat, up, down, and with my panting breath, out, in, the picture of a mother cat's stomach wet from suckling as it purrs long after the kittens have finished; and the music, oh, how I could hear that music, now, the beating of wild drums calling the female to the kill, his breathing swooning and winding through the key hole, under the door, over the door, sneering between the loose wood frame, lunging into the hard surface that wanted the ripe hard fruit, his breathing the music, his panting making me pant, making me want even more, for that I knew not of; I wanted to scream, from the pain in my breast, the pain rushing to the point, as the pain felt by a cats nail brushing against the leg in play while chasing the stray thread of a worn garment; the want of the take, the want to be suckled, to feel lips, tongue, and teeth upon swollen womanhood, upon tender pink meat never touched by any but the sponge for cleansing by my own hand and fingers when I rub the bleeding days pain from them, the ache I dreaded every month; and especially now, especially here, where an animal, other than my own hand, could touch me and dry the crevice wet with fearful desire, that I did not want to control; his breathing, his breathing, now at the door, opening the door, and welcoming me into the folds of purity and royalty.

Oh! I have gone too far, I should not be speaking of such things, this was not what I wanted to tell you; I allowed myself to be carried in the ecstasy of the moment.

This isn't what it is like always. No. One cannot respond the same all the time.

But this is not what I wanted to tell you; his secret, the secret.

Maybe I should not share it. Maybe it would put you into more danger. This whole speech has been.... I've endangered you with the little I have told. This must stop here.

No. I will not go further. I did not think this through. You are not ready. Ma was right to run; I see now it was not her that was weak, it is me! I understand! I have given in! I've never been in control!

What I talk about is something one must keep contained! I have failed! Ma knew she would not be able to contain herself and would lead another into what could kill! It is a world that few can live in, and I should not expose you, for you could fall into vicious jaws—there are others like him! I have spoken without considering the consequences to you! If you enter a world that only few can, and too quickly.... Oh, Lord, forgive me!

I can't answer why or for what.

Exhibit 3f: Letter to Uncle from Vlad, February 28, 1836

February 28, 1836

Dear Uncle,

My mate is and always will be the only Lady in the house. Once her transformation is complete, there will be no need to worry about finding another mate. No other mate could be more than she; nor complete me any better. To search many lives over, to test woman after woman, to watch them die at the refusal of their transformation—Uncle, you were right in saying, "Find one that is bred of us." Why not you; why not your own advice? There will be no danger of my closet becoming a memorial of failures. If I fail with Darling I will die!

In doing so, I will never need to keep a room of my failures. Thank you, Uncle: I can't imagine living with all your failures, with all your loves, lost to you forever, and forever seen! O! What a curse for our kind to carry; that we must keep the past hidden in front of our eyes; that we cannot depart from what we have done. I took your words wisely, Uncle, and please forgive me, as you foresaw, the taking of your daughter, by me. Reluctantly, you gave me your permission, if it should happen to be her (some part of me believes you preferred it was me). The first thing I will do for you, Dear Uncle, is let My Lady's mother know about the women she found in your past; but I do not believe that is why she ran, nor do I think you believe this. You do not want to face the obvious, she feared becoming one of them, she feared the children would be like you, and she knew she would die if she stayed. Is that why you let her go? You couldn't commit to another trophy in your closet? Cisci Loop has helped greatly in preparing Darling. More Priestess are needed. Less women would die. But she plays a dual role. Why do we trust her? How I wish you could answer these questions.

Your Dear Nephew Vlad Lyion

Exhibit 4b: Storyline: Secrets Are Not Secrets, October 01, 1836

Here are two pieces placed together, that supposedly took place on the same day as "Darling Speaks to Precious." As with the monologue, these two pieces are to be played out. While it is to be done similar to a "play" or more on the lines of a Native American storytelling event, this piece of evidence falls in line with the letters and other evidence presented.

Secrets Are Not Secrets

October 01, 1836
"My Precious, what was it you were running from?"
    "Mama?"
    "Tonight, in the woods, just off the trail?"
    "Something frightened me."
    Something? Darling hasn't spoken the truth to me; she frightened Precious; maybe for the better. Something did frighten her, yes, something, but it didn't chase her. And I was there to hear that something, to smell and see that something. Darling, how dare you spin the net of sensual want for a man! Your fear was nothing more than the hunt and kill. A sensual hunger that could eat you, eat right through your very soul! Lie to me! I lost you to the beast, but I will not lose Precious. Why did I let you go!? Maybe I can still save you. I must tell you of your

true father, the father known as Beast, which you only know about through stories of lies that I have made to protect you and your sister—and now! Forgive me for lying to you, to both of you; I only wanted to protect you and Precious. After this, you'll permanently leave the safety of the woodland that is more civilized than the world beyond this small state of affairs—what an awful world it is! At first, it was everything that it was supposed to be, until... I couldn't handle that secret I came across; the thought of knowing that.... I can't think about that now. I couldn't keep My Darling from falling into the trap I fell in, the trap that I found as a person, a trap that I have been unable to escape from, that she is unable to escape from, that I want Precious to escape from.

"Mama? What is wrong?"

"Nothing Precious. I was thinking of your sister."

"What is it that you are knitting?"

In my lap I see a jumbled pile of uncalculated stitches. "Nothing. Just practicing my stitching. Have you seen your sister?"

"She is with Cisci."

"Yes, yes, I remember now." Lie.

Mama is acting strangely. Did she hear us? And if she knew Mr. Lyion was... ? I cannot tell; for his hand upon my forearm was more than I could withstand; OH! that sensation, that exoticness that I read in Mama's letters. My nipples bursting from the bind, wanting his pant to run over my chest. I cannot think this way, I cannot allow myself to feel this way, it is so frightening, and so thrilling! What can I do? The gentleman that is often with Mr. Lyion watches me with interest. Darling isn't unaware. I fear sleep tonight; he comes to me in my dreams. I can still hear his call. To run into the wilderness and be lost forever to him! A man's touch is incredible. Why hasn't mama explained any of this to me?

But what am I to do with Mama? She knits without counting, changing patterns in the middle of a row. I don't think she is aware of what she does. Where was she that she knew I was running? that I was being chased? *or was I being chased but hunted*. Why does Mr. Lyion chase me as well? Does Darling know? Why did I lie? What does Mama know?

"Mama?"

"Yes Darling."

"Do we have enough sprouts to serve tonight?"

"Plenty. I brought up more from the garden. This warmth late in the season has been helpful this year. The garden is growing well, we won't be hungry this winter."

"I know mama. The greenhouse is a blessing, as well."

That smile on her face, what is My Precious thinking? I have to tell her tonight. I must confront Mr. Lyion, but what would I tell him that he would believe a woman's threat is severe? To expose him for what he is? It would shame my daughter as much, even more, than it would him. She would be tarnished, shunned from the community for being touched by a Beast.

Mr. Cougar, what did you do to me? What are my daughters? Beauties birthed for Beast? Mamma, why couldn't you protect me? You knew! You knew! Why can't I protect them? Darling Sister, you never had to worry.

"Precious?"

"Mama?"

"Bring me my chest."

"Your chest, mama? Whatever for?"

"There are things you need to know."

"Mama?"

"Go, My Precious."

"Yes Mama."

Mama knows. She knows I have been in her chest; she knows that I have been looking through those pictures and letters. I would love to visit my Aunty and Nanna. Why is she so scared of this Mr. Cougar? She loved him enough to make love to him! I want to know about my father. Will she tell me? What type of disorder did he have to make her go away? So many questions. I can't act too excited about getting the answers. Mama has guarded this all too well. Oh! I never replaced the key this morning!

Exhibit 2d: Telegraph to Adorra from Cherrish, March 01, 1836

This telegraph was found amongst the letters.

March 1, 1836 Dear Sister. I'm telegraphing you because we will be burying Mr. Cougar in two days. Is there a way you can come? Boston isn't far from you, by train. I think you should give your last departing words to Mr. Cougar. No women made him stray from your love. His last words, to me, were he wanted a family, to have a family with you. Since he is gone now, come on home. Mamma misses you, and so do I. Have you liked the pictures I've sent you? You have never mentioned them in the two letters you have recently sent. Mr. Cougar wanted you to have them; he took most of them himself, with the new type of photograph box. I've learned how to use it. I think there is money in this new product. I've strayed from the subject. Please come to Boston.
        Love,
        Your Darling Sister Cherrish

Exhibit 5b: Manifesto: Warning to the next tenant who enters Apartment F: time may not appear as be, March 12, 1835

This piece of evidence was found shoved in Miss Winter Woods' diary.

Warning to the next tenant who enters Apartment A: time may not appear as be Posted: March 12, 1835

When entering this room, forget the moment, remember the future, remember the past, do not attempt to feel or understand, just be.

Time invades life, filing the past in the present, the future in the past, the present left to stand alone unless it is one or the other. The night sky keeps the record of life. The moon is a cataclysmic anomaly thought to be from us, or us; it is all unknown. Living in the present can never happen, it is always fleeting, it is always the future first, then the past last; the two never meet.

On the walls, on four walls, posters, articles, advertisements run together and over each other, each from their own time, their own place, but never this moment, this happening. Only on the walls can Time meet each other, can the ends complete the circle, can the sky speak about what it sees over and through time. The stars write the words in the shadows on top of the walls plastered with human words. One flicker is a single letter speaking many words written and not yet written, many words that flee just as they are said and not thought of before the fleeting moment.

A fish crawls into the sky; the firework sleeps in the water. The psychotic face appears above the shepherd; the fire swallows the eye that is to see. Cosmic force controls nothing; the heart has no touch, only ache, only sorrow, only grief with a brief glimpse of joy when it believes the fingertips are connected to it. A fish with fangs flashes its bulb; the echo of fireworks blinded in a moment, not noticed, unseen, in the past, eaten for eternity. The lips speak to ears that listen like an eye; the shepherd cozies up to the fire knowing the words are whispers of tiredness, whispers of imagination, whispers of loneliness and the wilderness come to be known as home.

Beware of muddled Time that is sane.

As reported by Deloris Jaguer: Brief Clip; New Evidence, June 23, 2010

Brief Clip; New Evidence published in the late edition of a local paper on June 23, 2010. The defense keeps going back to the contract, wanting proof of such an endeavor to have a sheet of paper magically show words in red after a thumbprint of blood is placed on the paper. Today, the prosecutor brings in that speculation. The prosecutor places a willing subject on the stand. Her demeanor upsets the balance of the jury, the men either lowering their eyes or sniffing uncontrollably. Most of the audience squirms like worms trying to find their way into the soil to breathe properly. Her time is not our time. It isn't her clothing that tells us. It isn't her makeup. If you passed her on the street, she would be like any other women. As she sits there, her acquired shyness drops in her face. When her lips speak "thank you," a strange affect takes hold of the whole room. Even my ears pick out the "I can obey only if I so wish; it is you that will obey me." She states her name: Temperance Myngx. The prosecutor shows her a blank sheet of paper. He asks if she would sign her name. Before any objections can be made, she pricks her finger with a needle, squeezes blood out, places it on a blank sheet of paper, which then begins to *come alive* with words in red. The defense yells, "Objection!" The audience and the jury "oh" in surprise. Trick or Fact? I'm saying in my mind, *chemical testing*. I'm also wondering if this happens with anyone's blood. Is this only a manifestation in today's world with our technology? How can the prosecutor say such a display was possible hundreds of years ago? While I am skeptical, my mind thinks about pyramids, Stonehenge, and other sites such as these. What has our history lost?

Deloris Jaguer

Exhibit 2e: Letter to Adorra from Cherrish, March 15, 1836

March 15, 1836
Dear Sister,

You will find the photograph box enclosed in this package. Mr. Cougar's Will & Testament will be read March 4th.

Please come.

Love,

Your Darling Sister Cherrish

Exhibit 2f: Letter to Adorra from Cherrish, March 26, 1836

March 26, 1836

Dear Sister

Mr. Cougar left you everything! The house and all within it, the stables, the new business that he bequeathed me to run, as president! Sister, why is it that you ran, and do keep away? Can you not share your secret? Something had to be wrong. Every moment, every hour he spoke of you with love, nothing more. What was it that kept you away?

Love,

Your Darling Sister

Cherrish

P.S. Finalization cannot be completed until your arrival or that of your offspring. Come soon. Why would he request your offspring?

Exhibit 2g: Letter to Adorra from Cherrish, April 11, 1836

April 11, 1836

Dear Sister

I'm sorry to hear you feel that way. And in turn, I and ma, and my new husband thank you for the home, but we cannot keep it. We will send you rent money. Mr. Cougar made it very clear that the property could never be sold, and any heirs that you were to have would inherit the property. Mr. Cougar bought a law firm to secure this. Please come home and claim what has been given to you. In the meantime, Mamma and I will keep the place in shape.

Love,

Your Darling Sister Cherrish

P.S. The business keeps us real busy. Short letters will be my best. Come home.

Exhibit 8: Voice Recording, April 20, 1754

A recording found within Apartment D, dated April 20, 1754, a time when "tapes" did not exists, let alone anything to do recordings. Only one voice can be heard, a female, except for the screams that sound like a large male cat in pain. Is it possible that this tape was done during the 18th Century? The experts can't explain how this tape is in a metal box sealed by a lock all dating to the 1800s. The tape appeared to be in good condition, as if only placed in the box a few years ago. A note was left on top of the box: "By the time this is found, there will be instruments to use for listening."

rrrroooooooaaaagggrrrr.

"No, no, please, it's all well, please.

"Yes, I will call if I have need."

rrrroooooooaaaagggrrrr.

"Be silent I say. You called upon me, begged me to bring you in, said that you were at my mercy. This is my mercy. Be silent and learn the torture you have given me. To scream again will cost you your breath.

"Don't speak to me about love. It is only your lust for my blood. I've learned that much.

"You know the escort will not rescue you. You are under no protection here.

"Yes, the door must remain open, but there is no stipulation to what 'open' means: a crack or wide."

mmmmmeeeeewwwww.

"Don't whine. You want my attention. You have

it. Now, how does this feel?

"As I thought. Desirably wrong. Now, what about this?

"Good. Your silence allows the eyes to say more than any words. You will hate to love me.

"Understand, my training on the Eastern Front is wanted by many. It was only yesterday I saved a young boy's life by such an act I do upon you now.

"No. Don't yell out or I will keep the air from entering your lungs. All it takes is my index finger to cover the opening giving you life."

Exhibit 3g: Letter to Uncle from Vlad, May 30, 1836

May 30, 1836

Dear Uncle

I've been thinking over our last visit, before your death. Darling's mother knew my scent. I didn't lead on that I noticed. She leered at me when I spoke to her second daughter, Precious. (I must say she covered the smell of old pelt upon her flesh well—it has taken me this long to detect it.) You had to know. That's why you refused to look for another, to take another, Adorra is one of us.

I am sure Adorra left after her mother recognized who and what you are. Did you not know who her mother was? Of course you did, that is why you chose her. Especially after finding the others in the locked room, the fear of her mother's words overwhelmed her, she not wanting to be what her mother is, of wanting to be one of many loves kept.

Although, she did come to you one last time, she did love you. The first meeting with her, after secretly seeing her daughter, she smelled the hunt upon my sweat, her response a deep-throated growl, a growl of protection, of her territory, that I ignored, that I took as a clearing of the throat as she imitated illness from the new blooms.

How I wish I was not bound by my word; to not follow through would curse me and My Lady—I do not want your children to suffer, but I do not wish Your Lady to suffer either. Leopard is on his way. I see no other way to get Precious out of her mother's grip. Refusal of transformation is death, she is transforming now, her mother even refusing help from Cisci. No others come near, have been near to cause the transformation to begin. Could it be my presence?

I will be confronting Adorra as soon as Mr. Leopard arrives with Darling to finalize your Last Will & Testimony since Adorra will not go there.

Darling recently came to know you exist as father.

Vlad Lyion

Exhibit 2h: Letter to Adorra from Cherrish, October 13, 1836

October 13, 1836

Dear Sister,

I was surprised to see you open up. I will keep this news from Mamma, as you asked. But you must know, Mamma wants grandchildren, and if I told her she would stay off my back! Come home. I really need your help here. The business is crazy! Who did you marry? You did marry? Why didn't you tell Mr. Cougar and release him from his pain? Two girls: Darling and Precious. Lovely names. Boston is wonderful, so full of life, a wonderful place to raise children. Think about it, would you.

So happy to see letters from you; however, your letters worry me. Are you ill?

Love,

Your Darling Sister Cherrish

Exhibit 2i: Letter to Adorra from Cherrish, November 25, 1836

November 25, 1836

Dear Sister,

  Why so frantic? I'll do my best to change Alfred's mind about opening the door. Whatever is behind it? You sound frightened by it. Please tell me why. Come home so the door will never be opened and the secret of Mr. Cougar's will be kept. I'm sure you are right that Mr. Cougar never wished that door opened by anyone but him.

  Love,

  Your Darling Sister Cherrish

Exhibit 9: Journal of unknown, February 11, 1799

A single journal entry found on a wall, which, according to the old layout, is Apartment C in the old Bed and Breakfast: tenant unknown.

February 11, 1799
I am crazed like the animal rabid. These words come to me, and I must write. I know not what some of them are. Yet, I can see them, I know them, I have touched them, somewhere, somehow, and still,... I do not know any of it. Many days passed with myself feeling misplaced. I do not know why I am here at times.

There's that bark of the dog again. When I ask an escort about the dog barking, he replies, "What dog?" What dog indeed!

Here is what came today.

the dog barks madly my way

1.
the streetlight wears through the wet pavement
five uncovered fifty-four by fifty-six dining room
windows shiver
the red Dakota turns the table maroon

2.
the maroon table glances at me

              seven feet from the ground
i only shake my head as i go by
             the window
       the dog barks madly my way
the stove fan breathes lightly
       it isn't the garbage bin being dragged

        sighing
        vines hang from the half dead elm
     the overhead light blanches the white
           a raccoon's home
               a slice
of bright ebony swims under the windows
        business' lights sway with the tree
the dog barks madly my way
           the wind plays
      saplings of cattails overrun the garden
    fruit and nut trees surrounds the dog house

3.
i wait
    i shake   4.
    black doesn't return   garbage bin wheels
lock and scrape the gravel
i write   I look to see
    i sleep
I huddle on the couch between cushion and blanket
    i wake   the dog barks madly my way

        a house alone
        relatives outside
           relatives inside
       talking about dream
          little secret
             creaky board

5.

                floor built with books
synapses   mind built with books
   corpuscles   imagination built with books
      dance the brain   a spider hangs

a hammer drops   6.
     a foot screams   sanity
   the dog barks madly my way   saneness
a roof repair   causes the black
   standing on head
     husband's head   black invades
       space
         land
          sleep
            writing
              me

7.
two pastors watch
     each other
       me

a bull throws a horn
daylight plays with children
a slur haunts   8.
watching two pastors listening to me
      don't discuss this
listening to two pastors watching me
      nod and smile
      tell them to pray
a bull conceives outside its species
the dog barks madly my way   black is found
    a muse
      truth

                              a large stake
                    God between me
                    soul tampering
                    the black i have found

I've only been here for ten days and I have written more
than thirty entries such as these. I paste them upon my
walls. At least *He* is not entering my dreams anymore,
not even my waking dreams.

Exhibit 2j: Letter to Adorra from Cherrish, February 12, 1837

February 12, 1837

Dear Sister,

Do not worry, Alfred has given up on opening that door. Mamma was very forceful in persuading Alfred that the room was a sacred place and that Mr. Cougar would haunt him for disturbing it. I'm confused by Mamma's way. She seems just as frightened of that room as you do in your letters. What is behind that door?

Love,

Your Darling Sister Cherrish

Exhibit 2k: Letter to Adorra from Cherrish, June 27, 1837

June 27, 1837

Dear Sister,

Why did it take so long for you to tell me all this? What do you mean you are not married? Were you raped? Did you let yourself... go? I understand why you do not want mother to know. Were you having an affair with a married man while you were away? This is not you. What happened all those years ago? Maybe I have jumped to a conclusion, and you are a widow. Many widows do not speak of their dead husbands. It causes too much pain. I apologize for judging you. I have no right, I do not know what circumstances you were in.

Love,

Your Darling Sister Cherrish

As blogged by Deloris Jaguer: *The Nonfiction of Beasthood*: Video Interview with Victim, September 10, 2010

On the blog, *The Nonfiction of Beasthood*, by Deloris Jaguer, where you will find a video recording of an interview. A young lady, not married more than a month, just this past year, left her new husband based on what she saw in photographs taken of her husband holding the deer he had bagged. She currently resides in a sanitarium because her husband has had her committed.

Starlet:

I, [Starlet Clearwater], declare this video affidavit to be true and factual as I understand the situation presented to me twenty-three days after my wedding, and give Deloris Jaguer permission to use this video as needed to protect women from men such as my husband; I also give permission for this video to be used in a court of law. I do take this seriously. I am not crazy or delusional. I know there are other women out there, now; many are in the position I am now or fear for their lives every day. I can't imagine a woman accepting a man that is physically half wild— that is living a fantasy life if a woman believes it to be romantic. Those woman belong here instead of me. I would like to add, none of this is scripted. I will do my best to give the full details.

Deloris:

    Don't forget the date.

Starlet:

    Oh, this is being recorded September 10, 2010. It all started after developing the film my husband and I had taken for the past three months, which included our wedding, a very simple wedding—he insisted on nothing big and only a few people, with no actual reception: get married and take a week honeymoon. At first, I didn't think much about it as I scanned through the photos, looking at what we had done over the three months we had been together. I know people will say, "Only three months?" We had a mutual friend. We had communicated for about a year and occasionally went out to the same places with our friends but never made a connection until a month before we decided to get married. Hasty, I know. I realize that now. He just made me feel really comfortable. He enjoyed snuggling and nature, wasn't afraid to be adventurous. He was a man's man, as it is said. Anyhow, as I was saying, I didn't think much about the photos at first, thinking it was some strange lighting coming through the car window or a shadowing from something somewhere. I went through the rest of the photographs but never saw anything strange about them. Going back to the beginning, I looked closer, I noticed a shadowing across my husband's face. I moved the photographs about, lifted them to the ceiling and looked, took them under the dashboard to get rid of most of the light, and looked. Only the photographs with him and the deer were different, had that shadowing. The other photographs didn't have the ghostly image of a cougar obscuring his face. Yes, a cougar, or an Indiana mountain lion, some type of large cat from this area. I wanted to be logical; so, I thought maybe it was something in the area where the pictures were taken but couldn't understand how nothing else had the ghostly image covering it.

I didn't say anything to Lionel. I decided to show them to my friend first—our friend (wrong move, I know that now). Then, as I was cleaning and organizing our apartment, a small wooden trunk fell over, spilling out all sorts of paperwork and photographs. The brownish coloring of them made me think these papers were from his parents, at first. I started picking them up and putting them back into the trunk when one photo caught my attention. The photo was newer and dated a year before we met. Here he was with this same ghostly image across his face. I didn't understand; this frightened me. Finally, I was able to sit down with "our" friend. I showed her the old photo and the new photo. She said he probably arranged to have his photo taken that way.

A few days later, I ran into Lionel's hunting buddy. I asked him if something had been placed over the lens (though I didn't see how it would only effect my husband's face). I was told a standard camera with nothing added was used. I was shown the camera—standard it was. Before I confronted Lionel, I decided to look through all the papers in the trunk that had dumped onto the floor that day. In it I found other photos of him dating back to the early 1800s. Written on the back of a photo, again him with a bagged deer, was "Good day. I will be home soon. To my love, Precious. Lionel." The man looked just like my husband. The first name was the same. What was this? I thought maybe this photo had been doctored to make it look old and had the date added to make it look authentic but the feel of the photo paper told me differently. I'm no expert in photography but it isn't hard to spot "old."

I confronted my husband to have him only laugh at me like I was some child. He claimed it was his great great great great grandfather, or maybe five greats. His excuse for the ghostly image on the faces was dismissed with a wave of his hand, saying, "I don't know what causes that; it happens all the time when the Leopards hunt. As I kept asking questions, telling him what I had discovered, his face began to change before me—it was like watching those movies where a man changes into a wolf. I watched in horror and started to cry. Once he noticed the look on my face, he turned away. In short time, he had gone out the door and was lingering out back as I still stood there. As I collected myself, I went back to the closet, grabbed the trunk (you have to realize it was small), a few pieces of clothing, and left. I went directly to "our" friends. She had known him longer than anyone and would possibly have answers, I hoped. The first night there, I didn't say much. I went through the trunk. I found a certificate of birth, or what looked like one. Then I found another. Each name begin with Lionel. The only difference was the spelling of the last name. The last birth certificate was 1954 with Lionel Leapord: mother Florra Birch; father Leonard Leapord. The same father on each certificate. Florra Birch is the name of "the" friend. Why didn't I see it then? Why did I trust her?

She confessed to being his sister. She had been sent to another family member, on the Birch side. The family thought it fitting to name her after her mother. Something inside me didn't believe her but I had nowhere to turn.

Sitting here, saying all of this, my name fits right into the whole pattern of women: Starlet Clearwater. Thinking back on all those names... Beauty Grove,

Aurora Rainbow, Heavyn Lily, Krystal Peony.

Everything else happened very quickly. I'm not sure I understand how it all happened. I was committed to a sanitarium. Those photographs were never seen by anyone else. The friend, the sister, whatever she was, disappeared. I was told there wasn't any record of her. My husband said she never existed, and his friend, Timber Tigrell backed him up. Here I am, left in this place... however, it seems there are more women who have gone through what I did. They have names similar to mine. Their husbands' names are... similar—all familiar with a big cat. We can't all be nuts. I promised I wouldn't say their names because they are finally getting out of here after four years of confinement.

When I saw the news clip about the trial of a man who is accused of being something other than what he is, and read the clip in the newspaper, saw the women coming forward who had similar experiences but instantly ran, ran far far away, luckily enough finding out the strangeness before saying "I do," I realized I had a chance. Someone who did get out of here sent you to me; that is why I'm speaking to you today. And I noticed your last name. How did you come by it?

Deloris:

Let me say, I came involved in this endeavor because of my last name. My mother gave me my father's last name but I never knew him. As I have done research, I have found strange coincidences as you have just mentioned. While I carry my father's last name, there is no record of him, nor is he on my birth certificate. I legally have no father, only my mother's word on a man I have never seen. One last question. Does he know you had a child?

Starlet:
No. And I won't be telling him.

Deloris:
What about this video?

Starlet:
Guess I'll have to get a protective order, won't I? Or find a place to hide her—hopefully.

Deloris:
I'm sure he will return for her... legal guns blazing.

Starlet:
I can only ask for help from you and all others: protect my daughter!

Deloris:
Thank you for your time Miss Clearwater; nice to know he found a way to divorce you and you were able to regain your maiden name.

Exhibit 2l: Letter to Adorra from Cherrish, July 19, 1837

July 19, 1837
Dear Sister,

Your last letter was... I don't know what to say. No one would have known what Mr. Cougar was. Why did you not tell me? Tell Mamma? But you were wrong in not telling Mr. Cougar about the children, for they are his. No matter how much of a disorder he had, he was a man with a heart, more heart than a full-fledged man. I understand your fear of the girls becoming animal like in instinct, but don't you think living in the middle of nowhere, in the middle of a wild forest that it would make it prominent? The city does not contain the same hunt as the woods. I will pray for you.

Love,
Your Darling Sister Cherrish

Exhibit 2m: Letter to Adorra from Cherrish, October 01, 1838

October 1, 1838

Dear Sister

I'm sending the last letter. All funds due you for rent and profits will be done through a lawyer. I only wanted the best for you and your daughters; and regardless how you feel, your daughters will inherit everything. I'm sorry you feel as you do. I didn't send anyone to bring you home. I don't even know this Mr. Lyion! Someday I hope to see you and the girls. I have a son, Will. I will no longer take these accusations from you.

Love,

Your Darling Sister Cherrish

P.S. I do believe that Mr. Cougar had a nephew, which visited Mamma and I before Mr. Cougar died, sometime after you left the second time. Whom you describe sounds like that person. But he didn't say his name was Mr. Lyion, he called himself Detroit.

Exhibit 10: Letter to Lily from Blake, April 20, 1801

This letter was found intact inside the original envelop, unopened (the seal unbroken). This letter was found on the old site of the Bed & Breakfast.

777 Covington Way Boston, Massachusetts April 20, 1801

Lily Winterfield c/o Cisci Loop Bed and Breakfast 1 West 2nd, Apt. E Indianapolis, Ind.

Miss Winterfield: You Are a Woman Made for Beasthood,

We surround and penetrate your blood surging that escalates to power to become one with Beast. We are in your blood, directing the path it must take to serve the livelihood of Beasthood, the only tamed mortals that prowl the Earth. All of your refusal, your resistance, will not protect you from the touch placed upon you. We are near you always. Your blood knows us, recognizes us as the disease that cannot be lived without. Understand this: your blood cannot mingle outside the pride. Your life has no existence without us. You are ours; you are us; accept your path. We watch you move among others, shaking your foot, your leg, an arm, a hand. We see you dance when shopping in the Market Square, when attempting the pleasure of a man that isn't the blood. The world witnesses a woman of hysteria, a woman who cannot be taken seriously, a woman with wiles that cannot be met, a woman who knows nothing more than fancies. The men you acquaint yourself with leave soon, not knowing how to handle the scrawling you say you feel upon your skin. This will never leave, but can be squelched with Beast. Accept your fate.

Imagine a smooth finger tracing the scrawl from your neck to your thigh, the tongue that will caress the urgency sweltering in your bosom; a Beast can release your need far longer than the common man to allow a calm you haven't had since childhood. The Beasthood is the only drug your body can have, the only cure to bring pleasurable release before another surge of want, the only disease to combat the disease, to feed the hunger swollen in your body, your mind, your blood, your soul. One of us will feed you, stop running.

The Beasthood Your friendly neighborhood Beast, Blake Tigair

Exhibit 3h: Letter to Uncle from Vlad, October 06, 1838

October 06, 1838

Dear Uncle

I will fail in saving Precious. Cisci has attempted to console Adorra's fears. Now that Darling understands, she will be moving to Boston with me. Mr. Leapird keeps his distance as to not drive Adorra from Timberland. But time is coming near. Precious is becoming wrathful, acting out, viciously hunting, taking any man to subside the need, leaving them... exhausted and near death, then she has night terrors; she must be taken away for transformation by Cisci, soon. Darling and Cisci stand by, waiting. Adorra keeps the doors and windows locked, but this does not always stop Precious, and Precious is very swift, we cannot catch her when she is on the prowl.

I wish you were here.

I've kept my promise.

What happens after this will not include me. Your Lady will know where to reach us. Darling carries our first. This child should carry enough of the genes, if a female, that she'll be whole: no transformation needed.

Your Loving Nephew (who misses you)

Vlad Lyion

Note to me, September 25, 2010

This note was mailed to me, postmarked September 25, 2010. By the time I received it, Ms. Jaguer had vacated her home, said goodbye to her mother, and disappeared.

Slaiven,

Thank you for including me in the investigation. It seems a person can't run away from her destiny. The next time you see me... I'll say it this way: When you see me again, you'll understand even more than you do now, and you will see me again. This is what I found out about me through all of this.

You've seen the evidence. I do know that my research has led me to understand these Beasts have an exceptional intelligence level. As I have researched, I have come to know a few of these Beasts. Those few searched me out—not to harm me or to *take* me but to help me find other women who need protection. It seems every two or three centuries a woman like me is born to *protect*, to take on the role of *Priestess*. It's a dual edge to walk. There are those women who wish to *join* with Beast. I have much to learn. Something confused me, though—how was it that Cisci Loop had a name that didn't fit the pattern? There had to be meaning in that name. Anyhow, after me and the *men* had created a safe haven for these women being hunted, I went back to my mother to ask questions.

Her one reply was this: "I had hoped to break the cycle by naming you differently than others. History called for you to be named Deloris Lupus. I had seriously hoped the Beast had disappeared, and there would be no more need for us." My mother's name is Khronilia Luppei (loop pay).

All the best; till we meet again, soon; Deloris Loopit.

Here I am at the end of this part of the story. I don't know what more will happen or if anything will happen. I can only conclude, the original article name is the best way to end this part of the journey:

To All Beast: We're Aware of You!

Dawn Cunningham writes to explore herself, a situation, others ideas, and to find truth. Her writing comes out of the joy of oral storytelling taught to her by Gran'ma Ginny through the Native American tradition. Writing is her sanity. Recent publications are *Confluence, Healing Words: A Journey Through the Ladder UPP*, and *Poetry Quarterly*.

Thank you to the Wapshott Press sponsors, supporters, and Friends of the Wapshott Press.

Kit Ramage
Muna Deriane
James Wilson
Rachel Livingston
Kathleen Warner
Robert Earle and Mary Azoy
Kathleen Bonagofsky
Suzanne Siegel
Phil Temples
James and Rebecca White
Richard Whittaker
Debbie Jones and Steven Acker
Cynthia Henderson
Nancy Lilly
Jennifer Bentson
Patricia Nerad
Ann Siemens
Elaine Padilla
Laurel Sutton
John Grigor Bell

The Wapshott Press is a 501(c)(3) not-for-profit enterprise publishing work by emerging and established authors and artists. We publish books that should be published. We are very grateful to the people who believe in our plans and goals, as well as our hopes and dreams. Our new website is at www. WapshottPress.org. Donations gratefully accepted at www.Donate.WapshottPress.org.

www.ingramcontent.com/pod-product-compliance
Lightning Source LLC
Chambersburg PA
CBHW070530130626
46555CB00003B/1341